Good, the Bad, and the Goofy, The
By: Scieszka, Jon
Quiz Number: 8524
ATOS BL: 3.8   F   IL: MG

Word	GL
adjusted	4
bugle	5
calmly	5
chanted	5
constellations	9
dumped	4
dusty	3
imagined	3
nasty	4
perfectly	6
pouch	5
scrawny	5
stampede	4
truly	3
weird	6

THE GOOD, THE BAD AND THE GOOFY

The thundering herd was fifty yards away.

> *"Cattle stampede. Here's what we need:*
> *Time freeze when Sam waves his sock,"* I said.

Twenty-five yards and still running.

"Wave your sock," I yelled.

Sam threw off his shoe, whipped off his red sock, and started waving it as hard as he could.

The cattle charged closer.

The cattle kept charging.

Sam waved his sock.

Sam waved. The cattle charged.

We closed our eyes and prepared to be run over by a real Texas longhorn stampede.

Praise for the Time Warp Trio:

"Laugh-out-loud reading. . . . A true melding of words and pictures, and jolly good fun."
— *School Library Journal,* starred review

"Fans will gobble up the latest time-travel installment as they eagerly await the next one." — *Publishers Weekly*

THE TIME WARP TRIO

The Good, the Bad, and the Goofy

by Jon Scieszka

illustrated by Lane Smith

PUFFIN BOOKS

Title hand lettered by Michele Laporte

PUFFIN BOOKS
Published by the Penguin Group
Penguin Books USA Inc., 375 Hudson Street, New York, New York 10014, U.S.A.
Penguin Books Ltd, 27 Wrights Lane, London W8 5TZ, England
Penguin Books Australia Ltd, Ringwood, Victoria, Australia
Penguin Books Canada Ltd, 10 Alcorn Avenue, Toronto, Ontario, Canada M4V 3B2
Penguin Books (N.Z.) Ltd, 182–190 Wairau Road, Auckland 10, New Zealand

Penguin Books Ltd, Registered Offices: Harmondsworth, Middlesex, England

First published in the United States of America by Viking Penguin,
a division of Penguin Books USA Inc., 1992
Published in Puffin Books, 1993

3 5 7 9 10 8 6 4 2

LIBRARY OF CONGRESS CATALOGING-IN-PUBLICATION DATA
Scieszka, Jon.
The good, the bad, and the goofy / by Jon Scieszka; illustrated
by Lane Smith.
p.   cm.—(The Time warp trio)
"First published in the United States of America by Viking
Penguin, a division of Penguin Books USA Inc., 1992"—T.p. verso.
Summary: The Time Warp Trio find themselves in the Wild West of
yesteryear, rubbing elbows with cowboys and Indians.
ISBN 0-14-036170-7
[1. Time travel—Fiction.   2. West (U.S.)—Fiction.   3. Cowboys—
Fiction.   4. Indians of North America—Fiction.]   I. Smith, Lane,
ill.   II. Title.   III. Series: Scieszka, Jon. Time warp trio.
[PZ7.S41267Go   1993]   [Fic]—dc20   93-15136   CIP   AC
Printed in the United States of America

To my good, bad, and goofy brothers—
Jim, Tom, Gregg,
Brian, and Jeff

ONE

High noon.

A hot, dry wind blows across the prairie.

"Where the heck are we?" asks Cooky.

"Cheyenne country," says Cowboy Bob.

An arrow whizzes out of nowhere and sticks in the side of the chuck wagon. Cowboy Bob calmly pulls it out and looks at it.

"Yep. Cheyenne. I'll bet Sitting Bull and his braves are looking to rustle our cattle off the old Chillum Trail."

Cowboy Bob squints up at the ridge. Two hundred Indians on horseback stand ready to attack.

A flash of lightning. A clap of thunder.

Two thousand longhorn cattle start to moo and mill around behind Cowboy Bob.

Cooky blinks nervously. "What are we going to do, Bob?"

Cowboy Bob tugs on his white ten-gallon hat. "Circle up the wagons and get lunch started, Cooky." He eases his two six-shooters out of his holster. "I'll stop these Indians. Then I'll hold off the stampede. By the time the cavalry comes to save the day, I'll be ready for grub."

"Will the cavalry make it in time, Bob?" Cooky freezes. The background music swells. The scene fades to black.

AND WE'LL BE RIGHT BACK WITH OUR "SATURDAY NIGHT AT THE MOVIES" FEATURE, *COWBOY BOB TO THE RESCUE,* AFTER THESE IMPORTANT MESSAGES.

Fred grabbed the remote and turned the sound down. "Yes! Cowboy Bob is going to stop Sitting Bull and his Cheyennes from stampeding his cattle off the old Chillum Trail. Can you believe it?"

"No," said Sam, eating the last of the potato chips. "Because they've got it all wrong. Number one, Sitting Bull was not a Cheyenne. He was the leader of a Sioux tribe. Number two, the trail from San Antonio to Abilene was called the

Chisholm Trail. And number three, Cowboy Bob is just a bad character actor reinforcing mindless stereotypes."

Fred shook two cans of soda, looking for a full one. "Well, excuse me, Mr. Information. Thanks for spoiling the movie." Fred found a half-full can and emptied it. "I wonder what it was really like back then instead of boring old now."

"Thanks so much for inviting yourself over for the night and then calling my house boring," I said.

3

Fred gobbled a handful of popcorn.

"I didn't mean your house is boring, Joe. It's great. But summer vacation is getting boring. Wouldn't it be great to be real cowboys for just a little while?"

I thought about galloping across the prairie, firing off six-shooters, roping cattle, and sleeping under the stars. I pulled out a small blue book with stars and moons and twisting silver designs.

"Well, I *have* been reading a little more of *The Book*. And I think I found a spell we could use to get us out of any trouble. It's called the Industrial Strength Time Freezer Spell and—"

Sam jumped to his feet. "Oh, no you don't. If you two guys are going to go get stuck full of arrows and stampeded by cattle, you can leave me out of it."

Fred grabbed another handful of popcorn. "Oh, come on, you chicken. We've handled giants, dragons, wizards, and pirates. What could be so bad about being cowboys?"

I held *The Book* in my lap.

Sam adjusted his glasses like he always does when he gets excited. "Don't touch that book, Joe. Every time you do we get in trouble. Just

4

because your uncle is a magician doesn't mean we have to be."

"You think I don't know magic?" I said. "Let me show you the Power Broomstick Trick. I'll hold this broomstick and bet that both you and Joe together can't push me from this spot."

"No way. I'm not trying any tricks or saying anything until you put that book away."

"But what if we could wish for something safe like being cowboys for just twenty-four hours," said Fred.

"No. That wouldn't work," I said, leaning on the broomstick. "What you have to do is—"

"Wait! Stop! Shut up!" said Sam. "Don't say another word. I know exactly what's going to happen. One of you two wizards is going to say something stupid like:

Yippee Ki Yi Yippee, Yippee Ki Yi Yo.
Take us back to cowboys long, long ago.

"Then that stupid green time-traveling mist will start to swirl around and we'll be in big trouble again."

"That would probably work," I said.

Sam adjusted his glasses and stared at me.

"What did you say?"

A faint wisp of green mist began to curl out of *The Book*.

"I think that rhymed spell would probably work."

"Oh, no," said Sam.

The green mist swirled thicker and deeper.

"Oh, yes," I said.

The mist rose over our shoes, the couch, the TV.

"*Yeee haw!*" said Fred.

T W O

High noon.

A hot, dry wind blew across the prairie.

"Where the heck are we?" asked Fred.

"Nowhere," I said.

Fred, Sam, and I looked at each other. We looked around as the last of the green mist dissolved at our feet. No cowboys. No horses. No six-shooters. No cavalry. Nothing but scrubby cactus, bits of grass, and dirt as far as we could see.

"What happened? What did I say?" asked Sam.

"Your 'Yippee Ki Yi Yo' spell worked perfectly," I said.

"But that's crazy. I just made it up," said Sam. "How are we supposed to know how *The Book* works if it keeps changing how it works?"

Fred kicked at a cactus and sent up a cloud of dust.

"That's how it works," I said. "It always changes how it works."

"Oh, great," said Sam. "So how do we get home again?"

"That always stays the same. The only way to get back to our time is to find *The Book* in this time."

Sam looked around at the grass, the dirt, the

8

sun. "Oh, thank goodness. What a relief. I mean, it should be a snap to find *The Book* out here. You look under that cactus. I'll look under this one. And in about a hundred years we should be done!"

"Shhh," said Fred, holding up his hand. "Do you hear that?"

Sam and I listened.

"Yeah, I hear the vultures circling. They're fighting over who gets to be first to pick our bones," said Sam.

"Give me a break," said Fred. "You're the one who wished us here. There must be cowboys around here somewhere."

"Yeah, *The Book* has never been wrong before," I added.

"This is true," said Sam. "*The Book* has almost gotten us killed with King Arthur. *The Book* has almost gotten us buried with Blackbeard's treasure. But *The Book* has never been wrong." Sam looked up at the hot sun beating down on us again. "Remind me to thank your uncle Joe for giving you such a great birthday present . . . if we ever crawl out of this desert alive."

"Shhh. There it is again," said Fred. "Do you hear that rumbling?"

"Yeah, that was your stomach," said Sam. "You know, we could also die of starvation, or exposure, or sunburn, or hypothermia, or—"

"I hear it," I said.

"Coming from over there." Fred pointed to a reddish brown cloud of dust on the other side of a small rise.

"Cowboys!" shouted Sam. "We're saved! Come on!"

We ran up the rise and looked over the top. A swarming sea of brown was kicking up the cloud of dust we had seen.

"That's a lot of cowboys," said Fred.

"Those are cows," I said.

"Cattle," corrected Sam.

The sound of hooves and mooing grew louder. We could just see a few cowboys riding around the edges of the herd.

Fred waved his hat and yelled, "Over here, you guys!"

The noise grew louder. The running sea of horns and legs grew larger.

"I don't think you have to call them over," said Sam. "They seem to be headed right . . . uh . . . right toward us."

I felt the earth beginning to shake beneath us. "Maybe we should move a little over this way, guys." We started walking sideways. It didn't seem to make much difference. The herd kept stretching out in front of us. We walked the other way. Now we could see the cowboys on their horses trying to turn the herd.

"It's a whatchamacallit," said Fred.

I looked for someplace to hide. There was still nothing but cactus, grass, and dirt.

"It's a thingamabob," said Fred. "It's a . . . a . . ."

"*Stampede!*"
yelled Sam.

The wave of cattle thundered toward us. We could see their long sharp horns, hear their wild mooing.

"*Run*," yelled Fred.

"We'll never be able to outrun them," said Sam. "The herd's too big. Joe, what about that Frozen Time Spell?"

"The Industrial Strength Time Freezer?"

The cowboys whistled and yelled. The cattle mooed. The ground shook.

"Now or never," said Sam.

I tried to concentrate.

"Hickory dickory dock. The mouse ran up the clock.
Cattle stampede. Here's what we need . . ."

I stopped. The herd was only a hundred yards away, heading straight for us.

"What?" yelled Fred. "What do we need?"

"Something to rhyme with clock."

"Block, rock, sock!" screamed Sam.

The thundering herd was fifty yards away.

"Cattle stampede. Here's what we need:
Time freeze when Sam waves his sock."

Twenty-five yards and still running.

14

"Wave your sock," I yelled.

Sam threw off his shoe, whipped off his red sock, and started waving it as hard as he could.

The cattle charged closer.

Sam waved his sock.

The cattle kept charging.

Sam waved. The cattle charged.

We closed our eyes and prepared to be run over by a real Texas longhorn stampede.

THREE

The ground shook. We froze.

A cloud of heat and noise and dust covered us. It roared past us like a runaway train. And then . . . nothing. The rumbling stopped. I opened one eye, then the other. There was nothing to see but reddish brown dust swirling everywhere. I could hear a few cows mooing softly, and what sounded like water splashing.

"Are we in heaven?" asked Fred.

"This must be the Time Freezer Mist," I said.

Sam coughed. "No, you dimwits. The only thing frozen is your brains. We're obviously in the middle of a cloud of dust kicked up by a herd of cattle that somehow just missed trampling us to death."

"Maybe it was supposed to go 'Hickory Dickory dare . . . ,' " I said. "Or maybe 'Mickey Mouse had a house . . .' "

"Shhhhh," said Fred.

"Not again," said Sam.

We heard a squeaking, banging, and jangling noise.

"It's coming this way," said Fred.

We stared into the thick, swirling dust.

The squeaking and jangling grew louder and louder. A big ugly thing with a bunch of legs and five heads suddenly appeared.

"*Whoa,* you idjits! *Whoa!*" growled the thing.

The dust settled a bit and we saw a wagon pulled by four mules. A funny-looking guy with a scruffy white beard was the driver and the owner of the voice.

"Shoot howdy. What the heck you boys doing out in the middle of this godforsaken nowhere?"

"We're, uh . . . we're . . ." I remembered our last two adventures and the trouble we got into as time travelers. "We're . . . looking for cowboys," I said.

The wagon driver spit a disgusting brown stream of tobacco juice. "Durn good place you picked to look, pardners—smack in the middle of the Chisholm Trail." He laughed again. "Though next time, iffen I was you, I'd stand back a mite. Them doggies get running in a awful hurry when they smell water." He pointed and spit again.

The whole herd of cattle stood drinking their fill at a river behind us.

Sam absentmindedly cleaned his glasses with his sock. "You wouldn't happen to have a thin blue book decorated with stars, moons, and cryptic inscriptions on its cover, would you?"

"A book, you say?" The driver scratched his beard. "I seen a book once. Last year in San Antone, I think it was."

"I didn't think so," said Sam.

18

"Could you introduce us to the trail boss?" I asked. "Maybe he could help us."

"Naw, he ain't much on reading, neither."

"We don't need help reading. We want to be cowboys," said Fred.

The driver looked us over from his seat on the wagon. "You boys aren't in any kind of trouble, are you?"

"The truth is, we live in New York about a hundred and twenty-five years in the future," said Sam. "And we were just looking for something to do on a dull Saturday night, so we used a magic book to come back to this time. But we didn't tell you that because we didn't think you would believe it."

The driver spit and then burst out laughing. "You are one funny little dude. I cain't make out half of what you're saying. But you are one funny little Yankee."

"Cooky! Hey, Cooky!" A big man in full cowboy gear—hat, bandanna, chaps, boots, and spurs—rode up at a gallop. He reined his horse to a stop two feet in front of us. "What the h— is this? A church social? Stop the jabbering and

get your cussed butt and chow wagon up ahead and set up for the night."

"I'm on the way, Bob. Just stopped by to see if these boys needed a hand. They tell me they're from New York. They want to be real cowboys."

Trail Boss Bob looked down at us and then stepped his horse sideways. "I don't give a crusty cow patty if they're from the moon and want to be the King of England. I've got a thousand head of longhorn to drive up this trail. And I've got to get fifteen more miles through Cheyenne country before nightfall." The Boss gave us another look. "Let 'em ride drag with the Kid to work for their grub. I ain't paying no wages to train scrawny greenhorns. Real cowboys? *Yahhh!*"

Bob slapped his horse and galloped off, spraying sand and dust all over us.

Cooky leaned over and spit. "Now, isn't he a tenderhearted fella."

"I don't suppose he had a small blue book in that saddlebag," said Sam.

"Real cowboys," said Cooky. And then he laughed and laughed and laughed and spit.

"I didn't think so," said Sam.

FOUR

The next few hours lasted a lifetime. The Kid (who turned out to be just a year or two older than us) fixed us up with three scrawny ponies that looked like they escaped from the used-horse lot.

Fred fell off once. I got thrown four times. And Sam quit counting how many times he got dumped by his cross-eyed nag.

Once we finally figured out how to steer our reject ponies, the Kid explained what "riding drag" meant. Our job was to follow the herd, round up strays, and keep the slow cattle moving. What we really did was choke on dust, run blind into cactus, and smell the nasty smell that follows two thousand cattle wherever they go.

Trail Boss Bob came back every once in a while to try out new curse words on us.

"Keep 'em moving, you prairie-dog pellets.

You'll never be real cowboys that way." Bob smacked Sam's pony on the rump and sent him into another cactus patch.

When the sun finally sank, we staggered into camp.

"I'm starved," said Fred.

"I'm hungry, thirsty, dirty, sore, and too tired to list everything else I am," said Sam.

We walked up to the campfire and joined about ten other cowboys around the chuck wagon. Cooky stood in the middle, dishing dinner out of a big iron pot over the fire.

"Hey, lookee here—it's our New York cowboys." Cooky spit a stream of tobacco juice, then plopped a spoonful of something on a plate.

The crew turned to check us out. They didn't look anything like Cowboy Bob on TV. Four of the guys were black, three were Mexican, and they were all even dirtier than we were. Most had scraggly beards and beat-up brown hats. They all had boots with spurs, bandannas around their necks, and jeans. Most had a single six-shooter in a holster. Nobody said a word. The sun slipped below the horizon and lit the clouds red and purple.

"Sit down and eat up," said Cooky, spooning up three plates.

"I think I'll just stand," said Sam.

Fred pushed the stuff around on his plate and smelled a forkful. "What is it?"

"Cooky only knows two meals," said a cowboy missing a few teeth. "So it's either bacon, beans, and biscuits or biscuits, beans, and bacon."

The rest of the cowboys laughed and hooted.

I tasted a little bite. It reminded me of some of our science experiments—like the one where we grew mold on bread and forgot about it for three weeks.

"I'll never complain about cafeteria food again," said Fred.

But we were all so hungry we ate the mess. We even sopped our plates clean with biscuits like everybody else. The last of the sunlight disappeared and a cool breeze picked up. We moved closer to the fire.

Fred took off his Tigers hat and tried to slap the dust off it. "What a life. What do you guys do for fun?"

None of the cowboys said anything. I didn't

want this time trip to be a repeat of our last two near-disaster adventures, so I spoke up, trying to sound as friendly as I could, in a cowboy sort of way.

"Howdy. My name is Jumping Joe. This here is Wild Fred. And that there is Yosemite Sam."

A few guys looked at us. Somebody burped. I figured I'd better keep talking before the beans took effect.

"We just want to say thanks for letting us join up with you. We'll only be sticking around a few days until we get to town and—"

"Two months, more like it," said Cooky, spitting into the fire.

"Two months?" said Sam.

"Yep. Take us at least that long to get to Abilene."

"Two months?" said Sam. "I can't take two months of dust and beans and bacon. We've got to get out of here." Sam jumped to his feet and chanted a spell:

> "We are rubber.
> Cowboys are glue.
> Send us back home.
> Whoop whoop-ee-do."

I sat Sam down and whispered, "Knock it off. They'll think we're crazy. Besides, the only way we can get back is to find *The Book*."

I had just managed to calm Sam down when Fred spoke up.

"And where are all those famous cowboys like Buffalo Bill and Wild Bill Hickok and General Custer?"

The biggest, meanest-looking black cowboy suddenly looked up. "Did you say Custer?"

"Uh . . . yeah," said Fred.

"There's a Lieutenant Custer at Fort Dodge leading the Seventh Cavalry. I just got out of the Tenth."

Then it suddenly dawned on me just where and when we were. "You mean Custer's still alive?"

"Last I heard."

"What year is this?"

The cowboys around the campfire looked at me like I was crazy. "Sixty-eight."

"Custer's Last Stand isn't until 1876," I said. "He attacks a huge camp of Sioux and Cheyenne. He and the whole Seventh Cavalry get wiped out."

Now the cowboys looked at me like they *knew* I was crazy.

"We've got to warn him," said Fred. "Where are they?"

"They're around here somewheres," said the cowboy from the Tenth. "They're looking for Black Kettle and his Cheyenne braves after what they done to them boys driving the King Ranch herd through here last week."

A coyote howled in the dark.

Sam's eyes almost bugged out of his head. "Wha . . . wha . . . what did they do to them boys driving the King Ranch herd through here last week?"

"First they tied 'em up. Then they scalped 'em," said Cooky. "Then they cut 'em open. Then they took their guts and—"

"*Cooky!*"

Sam and I jumped into each other's arms.

Trail Boss Bob appeared out of the darkness.

"Stop flapping your gums, you sorry sacks of sod. We've got trouble."

"Indians?" I asked.

"Worse," said Bob. "Thunderstorm. One crack of thunder and this Lazy J herd is gone just like this afternoon. Once a herd spooks, they'll spook again." Bob looked at Fred, Sam, and me like we were something he stepped in. "And when two thousand head of cattle run over a man, they don't leave much to bury."

"Thanks for sharing that with us," said Fred.

"Jake, you and Cody go on first watch. Try to calm them doggies down," growled Bob. "The rest of you be ready to ride."

We tried to find a comfortable spot on the

rocky ground. The sky was pitch black. Not a star to be seen. We could hear the cattle moving and Jake and Cody singing to them to keep them calm:

"Oh, slow up, doggies, quit moving around.
  You've wandered and trampled all over the ground.
  Oh, graze along, doggies, and feed kinda slow
  Hi-o, Hi-o, Hi-o."

Sam bumped his head on a rock. "*Owww*. Okay, Boy Wizard, it's been just swell being a real cowboy. But now I think we should find *The Book* and go home."

"But nobody here has any kind of book. Maybe it's in Abilene, at the end of the trail," I said, thinking out loud.

"I can't stand two months of that jerk Bob," said Fred. "We have to take our horses and get out of here tonight."

"Are you crazy?" said Sam. "There are Indians out there. Didn't you hear what Cooky said? First they tied 'em up. Then they scalped 'em. Then—"

"Yeah, but the Seventh Cavalry is out there," said Fred.

"So?" said Sam.

"So they probably have *The Book*," said Fred.

I thought about it for a minute. "Hey, Fred might be right. The cavalry always comes to the rescue. They must have *The Book*."

"That settles it," said Fred. "We escape tonight and find the Seventh Cavalry."

"Not me," said Sam, rolling up tighter in his blanket. "I'm staying right here and letting the Seventh Cavalry find me."

"Escape," said Fred.

"Stay," said Sam.

"Escape."

"Stay."

A streak of lightning and a sharp *crack* of thunder stopped any further discussion.

We felt a familiar rumbling through our blankets. We knew what it was before we heard Cody's yell.

"Stampede!"

FIVE

I thought the first stampede was bad, but this was worse, times twenty. In the pitch blackness Fred, Sam, and I rolled out of our blankets and started running. This was not a good idea because the ground suddenly disappeared. In the next lightning flash we found ourselves in a pile at the bottom of a gully.

We could hear the cattle mooing and running all around us. Cowboys yelled, whistled, and fired their guns trying to turn the herd in a circle. We could smell the cattle. We could even feel their heat. But we could only see the wild scene when the lightning flashed. Then it started to rain. Hard.

"Stay close to the bank," yelled Fred. "We'll be safe there."

Sam and I didn't need any directions. We were already trying to dig ourselves into the side so we wouldn't get squashed by any falling cows.

The ground shook and rumbled all around us. Lightning, thunder, and sheets of water crashed down on us from above.

Then I heard a different, *whooshing* kind of sound.

"What's that?" yelled Fred.

"I don't know," I yelled back.

The lightning flashed. I saw us standing in ankle-deep water.

The *whooshing* sound grew louder.

The lightning flashed. I saw the water moving.

The *whooshing* sound grew louder still.

I suddenly figured out what was making that sound.

"Sam! Fred! Climb! We're standing in a riverbed!"

We had just enough time to look at each other and scream before a wall of water roared around the bend and knocked us off our feet. We tumbled head-over-heels, every-man-for-himself for what seemed like miles.

Every now and then lightning flashed. I could
see Sam's head bobbing ahead of me. I could
hear Fred yell. I dog-paddled, jumped, and
bumped my way along. Brush, sticks, and what

32

looked an awful lot like dead lizards and snakes tumbled by. Thunder crashed. The rain slashed. The river *whooshed* along. And then, just as suddenly as it began, it was over.

The rain stopped, and I found myself floating in a quiet pool. I looked up and saw black clouds racing off, a few stars left behind. The sky lightened along one edge and dimmed the stars.

"Sam. Fred," I croaked.

No answer.

I paddled to the edge of the pool and crawled up the sandy riverbank.

"Sam. Fred."

I dragged myself to the top and looked around. Everything was the same, but everything was different. The same sand, grass, and cactus were still there. But there were no cowboys, no cattle, and worst of all—no Sam or Fred anywhere in sight.

I called, "Sam, Fred," one more time. Then I must have passed out because when I came to, someone was shaking me.

I was sure it was Custer and the cavalry come to the rescue. "Sam, Fred, we're saved."

I opened my eyes.

I saw moccasins, leggings, a beaded shirt, and a reddish brown face topped with a single feather.

I passed out cold again.

SIX

I woke to the jolting step of a horse. All I could see was the ground rushing past a beaded moccasin toe. It took me a minute to figure out that I was facedown over the horse's back, being carried off by an Indian brave. My hands and feet were tied together and I felt like I had been beaten all over my body with a large stick.

I tried to get the attention of my new friend.

"Excuse me. Hi. Hello there. Yoo-hoo. How?"

The brave reined his horse to a stop.

"Oh, thanks," I said. "Listen, I feel like I've been beaten all over my body with a large stick. Do you think we could maybe stop for a minute?"

The brave gave me a look, then jerked up my hands. I slid off the horse and landed with a thump.

"Ouch. Thanks."

The brave jumped off his horse. He wore some kind of hide leggings and a long-sleeved hide shirt with beads and fringe down the arms. A single feather was fixed kind of sideways in his long straight black hair. He carried his bow and arrows on his back, a long knife in his belt, and a rifle in his hand.

"Uh . . . hi," I said. I was so scared I could barely squeak.

He stared at me with the blackest eyes I've ever seen. I thought about the King Ranch boys.

"M-m-my name is Joe," I stuttered. "And I'm not really a friend of any of those cowboy guys. Nope. I hardly know them. I'm from another time, you see, and—"

The brave turned suddenly. He slid his rifle into his saddle. He took something out of a pouch and then eased his long, sharp knife out of its sheath.

"Oh, no," I said. "You can't scalp me. My parents would kill me."

The brave took a step toward me.

I put my bound hands on top of my head. "But I need my scalp."

The brave crouched in front of me.

"I know magic. I'll show you magic. Look—nothing up my sleeve."

The knife; the huge, sharp, shiny knife flashed quickly in the sun. It sliced a piece of something the brave held. He popped the stuff into his mouth, sliced another piece, and handed it to me. It was food.

I didn't know whether to laugh or cry. So I took the stuff and ate it. It tasted like old sneakers mixed with bacon fat and rotten berries.

"*Umm*. Good," I said, rubbing my stomach. "Delicious." I was so happy to still be alive with my own hair on top of my own head that I couldn't stop talking. I talked while we ate more of the nasty stuff. I talked while he cut the straps on my wrists and ankles. I talked while he hoisted me up on the bare back of one of the three horses he was leading. And I talked while we rode over miles of more sand and cactus. We finally rode up a hill and the brave held up his hand for quiet.

On the other side of a river stood a whole city of tipis. There must have been a hundred of them.

A small pack of kids and dogs met us as we crossed the river. The kids laughed and pointed at me, calling, "*Wasichu. Wasichu.*"

I waved back to them. "Hello. *Wasichu*. Hello. *Wasichu.*"

The brave and all of the kids laughed. I didn't see what was so funny. We rode past women scraping hides and cooking, men sewing hide shields and sharpening spears. Everyone stopped to stare as we rode by.

"Hello. *Wasichu,*" I waved. Everyone laughed again.

We rode up to a large tipi with dogs and scenes of battle painted all over it. A large, fierce-looking brave came out of the tipi. The kids and the dogs scattered.

"Another of the strange little *wasichus* for you, Bull Bear," said my guard in perfect English.

Bull Bear smiled a nasty smile. I stared in surprise.

"But I must warn you: I think this one's name is Talks Like the River. He never stops."

Bull Bear lifted me off my horse like I was a stuffed toy. He carried me into the tipi under one arm and dumped me on a pile of buffalo robes.

"Ow," said one robe.

"Hey, watch it," said another.

Sam and Fred appeared from under the buffalo robes.

"Sam! Fred! Am I glad to see you."

"Joe! Oh, man, are we glad to see you."

My eyes slowly adjusted to the light inside the tipi. Bull Bear sat on the other side of the fire pit, staring at me very intently.

"Why is he staring at me like that?" I whispered.

"He's glad to see you, too," said Sam.

"What?"

"Yeah," said Fred. "You see, when they caught us we kind of told them they had to find you, too. We said you were the one with the strong medicine."

"Strong medicine?"

"Yeah, you know," said Sam. "Magic."

"Strong medicine tonight," said Bull Bear. "No medicine—you die."

"Strong medicine?" I asked.

"That's right. Strong medicine," said Sam. "Tonight."

"Tonight?" I asked.

"Or we die," said Fred.

SEVEN

Bull Bear's wife thought we looked hungry. She brought us more of the rotten-sneaker meat stuff.

"Doesn't anybody in this time eat regular food?" said Fred.

"You were expecting buffalo pizza?" asked Sam.

In between halfhearted bites, Sam and Fred filled me in on what they had found out.

"These guys are from Black Kettle's Cheyenne tribe—the one Cooky said Custer has been chasing around," said Sam.

"Yeah," said Fred. "And the good news is that Black Kettle is not a bad guy. He wants to return us to Custer's cavalry to prove that they are a peaceful tribe."

"But the bad news," said Sam, "is that this guy Bull Bear is the leader of a group of warriors

41

called Dog Soldiers. He thinks they should return just our scalps."

"So let me guess," I said, feeling sicker than the food. "The council tonight is to decide whether they send back us or our scalps."

"Right," said Sam.

"Right," said Fred.

"Great," I said.

The council tipi was the largest tipi of all. Inside and out, it was covered with pictures and designs. A few stars twinkled in the bit of sky we could see through the smoke hole at the top.

Bull Bear sat Fred, Sam, and me in front of him.

A circle of old men and young warriors went all around the fire at the center. One guy sat in a special seat behind a circle of sticks. He held a bundle wrapped in fur and decorated with feathers. I figured he must be Chief Black Kettle.

Sam nodded toward him. "That's the medicine chief."

A friendly-looking old guy who reminded me of my grandfather stood up next to him. Everyone quieted down.

"Chief Black Kettle," said Sam.

"Brothers. We meet tonight to decide what to do with these three *wasichu* boys we have found. Let us now ask Grandmother Earth, Grandfather Sky, and the Four Directions for wisdom in deciding what is best for the People."

The entire tipi full of braves became instantly quiet. We sat as still as possible. I thought of all of the cowboys and Indians I had seen in movies and on TV. I thought of how far away from all of that we were.

"*Hiy,*" said Black Kettle, breaking the spell.

Everyone answered, "*Hiy.*"

The medicine chief unfolded the bundle. He

43

pulled out a red clay pipe with a long wood stem, and lit it with a stick from the fire.

The pipe passed from person to person around the circle. When it got to me I tried to look like I knew what I was doing. I puffed carefully and blew out a cloud of sweet-smelling smoke. I held back a cough and passed the pipe to Sam.

When everyone had smoked, Black Kettle spoke.

"Everyone here knows me and my thoughts on this. The White War Chief has promised to protect us if we follow the peaceful way. If we return these boys to the Bluecoats, they will know our hearts are good. If we kill these boys, it can only bring bad medicine and war to the People. It is I, Moka-ta-va-tah, that says it."

"Yeah," said Fred.

Bull Bear stood up. "Black Kettle, you have spoken, but you have also forgotten. You have forgotten my brother, our chiefs White Antelope, War Bonnet, and Yellow Wolf, and half of your tribe—all wiped out by the Bluecoats at Sand Creek three winters past. You have forgotten your own wife—shot by the same Bluecoats. Yes, we are at war. And Bull Bear and his Dog Soldiers

44

will fight until there are none of us left. Send the Bluecoats three scalps."

"Oh, no," moaned Sam.

After Bull Bear and Black Kettle spoke, just about everyone gave their opinion of what to do with us, most of it in Cheyenne. But it wasn't hard to figure out what they were saying. The older guys were mostly with Black Kettle. The younger braves were with Bull Bear.

More braves spoke.

The pipe circled around once more.

More braves spoke.

I was beginning to get dizzy with all of the smoke and talk when Sam leaned over. "Hey, I get it," he whispered. He pointed over behind the medicine chief. "This whole tipi is like a planetarium."

Suddenly everyone was quiet and seemed to be looking at us. Sam slowly lowered his pointing finger. "Uh-oh."

The medicine chief stood up and gestured to Sam. I think he said, "Would you like to share your joke with the rest of the class?" in Cheyenne. Two braves grabbed Sam and dragged him toward the fire.

"I'll never whisper in class again," said Sam.

But it didn't look like he would ever get a chance to keep that promise.

EIGHT

The two braves stood Sam in front of the medicine chief.

He raised a stick decorated with three feathers and pointed it at Sam. "Now you speak."

"Well, I was um . . . er . . . ah . . . just telling Joe here that your designs look a lot like constellations."

The medicine chief looked at the designs and then back at Sam.

"Constellations. You know . . . stars." Sam pointed to the biggest circle. "See—if this is Polaris, the North Star, then this is the tail of Ursa Minor, or the Little Bear." Sam traced the pattern of the Little Dipper on the side of the tipi. "Then this is Ursa Major or the Big Bear pointing toward the North Star, the one star that appears never to move."

"The Star That Does Not Walk Around," said the medicine chief, looking a bit surprised. "You know the stars?"

"Of course," said Sam, stepping around a few braves. "Astronomy is a fascinating and useful science." He pointed to a design of seven stars. "We call these the Pleiades. But you probably know them as the Seven Boys Who Danced Themselves into the Sky."

Now the medicine chief looked positively awed. "No *wasichu* has ever read my star designs." He sat down with a stunned look and began searching through the pouches and robes. The rest of the council looked equally stunned.

"He really is Mr. Information," whispered Fred.

Then Bull Bear stood up. "Every child in the village has heard the tales of the Great Bear and the Dancing Boys by the winter campfires. That is not strong medicine."

A few braves nodded. I looked around and saw we were losing votes, and maybe our scalps. Then I saw the medicine man's staff and had a stroke of inspiration. The Power Broomstick Trick. I hadn't actually had a chance to try it out yet. But I figured it was truly now, in 1868, or never.

I stood up. "My name is Joe the Magnificent. I have strong medicine."

Bull Bear gave me a look that could kill.

"I have medicine that will make Warrior Fred stronger than your strongest warrior."

Everyone began talking at once.

"Joe, are you nuts?" said Fred.

I walked to a clear spot in the center of the tipi and dragged Fred with me. "If I may use your staff."

The medicine chief nodded. I picked up the feathered staff and handed it to Fred. "Hold it horizontally, two hands on top," I whispered. "The trick is to pull up slightly when they push. It redirects their force."

"Are you sure?" whispered Fred.

"Sure I'm sure," I lied.

I tried to think of an impressive sounding spell. I waved my hands over Fred and chanted:

> *"Humpty Dumpty sat on a wall.*
> *Humpty Dumpty had a great fall.*
> *Now no brave can push Fred at all."*

49

Bull Bear himself stepped forward. The muscles on his broad chest and huge arms bulged in the flickering firelight. It was too late for second thoughts, but I was having them anyway.

Bull Bear grabbed the staff with a smile and pushed.

Fred didn't move.

He pushed harder.

Fred still didn't move. A few braves murmured.

He pushed as hard as he could, puffing and blowing.

Fred stayed right where he was.

Bull Bear dropped his hands with a look of disgust and the entire tipi roared. Sam cheered. Fred flexed one arm. I tried to look as magical as possible. Black Kettle stood and held up his hand for quiet.

"As your chief, I say we have a sign as clear as the stars above." He put his hands on my shoulders and smiled. "Truly these three small *wasichus* have come with good hearts to bring such strong medicine to the People. Tomorrow they shall be returned to the Bluecoats."

The crowd in the tipi stood up and walked out, talking among themselves. A few glanced sideways at me, Sam, and Fred. The younger braves didn't look too happy. The medicine chief made his way over to Sam. "I have something that is yours."

Bull Bear put one large hand on Sam's shoulder, one large hand on my shoulder, and squeezed Fred between us. "Now we sleep. Talk later."

Black Kettle gave Bull Bear a look. "You will take care of our guests?"

"The Dog Soldiers found them. The Dog Soldiers will take care of them."

"It is done," said Black Kettle, but he didn't sound too sure. Neither was I.

Bull Bear herded us out into the night. Black Kettle and the medicine chief stood together in the middle of the council tipi. "Tomorrow," said Black Kettle.

"Let's hope so," said Fred.

51

NINE

Bull Bear pushed us roughly into his darkened tipi. He was not in a good mood. Fred, Sam, and I sat on a pile of buffalo robes.

"Where did you learn that stick trick?" asked Fred.

"Just a little magic I picked up in a book," I said.

"And Sam, how did you know all that constellation stuff?"

"Just a little magic I picked up in a book."

Bull Bear fed the fire with a handful of grass and sticks. It blazed up and sent weird shadows dancing around on the inside of the tipi. He stared at us with a familiar nasty look.

"Didn't his mother ever tell him his face might freeze that way?" whispered Sam.

Four braves, all painted with the same red stripe

design across their mouths and eyes, stepped inside and sat down. Soon they were all talking
very excitedly.

"I think we better come up with some more
tricks or a certain book," said Fred. "Because
this does not look good for the visiting team."
We each found a robe and rolled up in it. "We
better keep an eye on these guys."

"Right," I yawned. "You and Sam sleep first.
I'll watch, then wake you up for your turn."

Sam was already snoring. Fred yawned,
"Okay," and rolled over.

The braves talked quietly now. One by one
they slipped out until only Bull Bear was left
staring at the dimming fire. I snuggled in the
warmth of the buffalo robe. I rested one eye for
a second. I rested the other. I rested both, then
opened them. Bull Bear was still there.

I rested one eye. I rested the other. The next
thing I knew I was being lifted up in the air and
carried. My mouth was covered. My hands and
feet were tied. I saw Sam and Fred being carried
along by more red-striped warriors. The sun was
just coming up as we were thrown over horses
and carried out of the village. I had no idea where

we were headed, but I had a sinking feeling it wasn't back to the cavalry.

We rode for hours, bouncing along on horseback. Bull Bear and his fierce-looking Dog Soldiers finally stopped and dumped us on the ground. One of the braves tied us to a twisted little tree.

"This does not look good at all," said Sam.

"Yeah," said Fred. "Remember Cooky said first they tied 'em up. Then they—"

"I know. I know," I said. "Don't remind me. I'm trying to think of something magic."

One of the Dog Soldiers rode up and pointed over the next hill.

Bull Bear smiled. He slid out his knife. "Let us see your strong medicine now, *wasichus*. Or maybe you will save it to show your cowboy friends." He pointed toward the next hill. I could hear the faint sounds of cattle mooing and someone, probably Cody, whistling and singing.

"I will cut a nice circle scalp," said Bull Bear, waving his knife in front of us. "When the cowboys see you, they will know you were scalped by Bull Bear and his Dog Soldiers. Then we will wipe them out and scalp them for the Bluecoats to see, too."

Sam, Fred, and I all strained against the ropes together, struggling to escape. It was no use. There was no magic, no trick, no book that could possibly save us now.

Bull Bear reached for Fred's hair. An arrow whizzed out of nowhere and stuck in the tree. Bull Bear stopped and looked up.

A pack of Indians on horses came screaming down the hillside. It was Black Kettle and the medicine chief, followed by at least thirty warriors. Black Kettle's braves whooped, screamed, and knocked heads with their war clubs. The ten or so Dog Soldiers were rounded up in a quick tussle and brought in front of Black Kettle.

The medicine chief sliced us free with his knife.

"Saved by the good guys," said Sam.

Black Kettle and Bull Bear stood face to face. Black Kettle was giving him a fierce lecture in Cheyenne. Bull Bear seemed to be making some kind of excuse, but Black Kettle didn't look like he was buying it. Black Kettle gave him one more blast and a hand gesture, then walked over to us.

"I must apologize for the actions of some of our warriors. There are always those who act first and think later."

"Oh, that's okay," said Fred. "My dad says I do that all the time."

Sam and I laughed.

A familiar-looking cloud of dust and the sound of mooing longhorns rose over the hill in front of us. I never thought I'd be so happy to see that dusty, stinky bunch of cows again.

"We will return you now to your friends," said Black Kettle. "And hope this may help you find your way home, as your return may help my people find the way."

Bull Bear and his Dog Soldiers scowled at us. The medicine chief pulled a fur pouch from his pony's saddle and handed it to Sam.

"And we return this to you, young watcher of

the stars. It has been with our Sacred Arrows for as many winters as I know. Perhaps you know also what these other strange markings mean."

Sam opened the pouch. We saw the silver stars and moons on a dark blue background and let out a yell just as the bugle blew its first blast.

"*The Book,*" yelled Fred.

The bugle sounded again and I saw where it was coming from—an army of hundreds of blue-coated soldiers, guns firing and sabres flashing, charging down the hill directly at us.

We were about to be saved by the cavalry, whether we liked it or not.

TEN

The bugle sounded the charge again.

Rifle shots cracked and bullets whistled over our heads.

Fred waved his hat and ran toward the charging cavalry. "Wait. Stop. These are the good guys. They're bringing us back."

"Stop, Warrior Fred," yelled Black Kettle. "Even your medicine is not strong enough to fight Bluecoat rifles."

The soldiers kept charging, whooping and shooting the whole way. Seeing they were hopelessly outnumbered, the Cheyenne braves jumped on their ponies and dashed up the opposite hill.

Buzzing bullets clipped a branch from the tree

and sprayed little explosions of sand at our feet. Fred waved his hat once more and then pulled it down. A bullet hole went right through the middle of the white D. "Yikes. These guys aren't kidding!"

Black Kettle kicked his pony into a gallop and in one smooth move leaned over, scooped up Fred, and dropped him on horseback behind him. The medicine chief hoisted Sam onto his pony. Another brave lifted me. And we galloped after the retreating warriors.

We had just reached the top of the hill when we abruptly stopped. Bull Bear and the rest of the warriors had turned their ponies to face back toward the cavalry.

"Don't stop now. Let's get out of here," I said. Bull Bear pointed over the hill. Two thousand head of Lazy J cattle stretched across the plain, blocking our escape ahead. I looked back. A hundred soldiers galloped past the little tree, blocking our escape behind. We were trapped.

Bull Bear and his Dog Soldiers calmly dismounted. They readied their bows and arrows. Some chanted. Others sang their death songs.

Fred, Sam, and I slid off the backs of our ponies and dove behind the nearest bush.

Bull Bear stood tall, testing the point of an arrow with his thumb. "Today is a good day to die."

"I don't think so," said Sam. He handed me the fur pouch. "Quick, Joe, *The Book*. Use it!"

I pulled the thin midnight-blue book from the pouch. Bullets stung the ground all around us.

"Those guys are trying to kill us," said Fred.

I looked at the cavalry charging up the hill. Their leader looked familiar in a history-book sort of way. I could just make out a "7" on the red-and-white banner. "Hey, I think that's Custer," I said.

"Maybe we can chat later," said Sam. "Right now he looks busy getting ready to make this *our* Last Stand."

"Yeah, come on already," said Fred. "Open *The Book* and let's get out of here."

I looked again at the Lazy J herd behind us, Custer and his troops in front of us. Then I looked up at Black Kettle. He didn't look particularly worried or mad, just kind of sad. Dust and noise swirled all around us. Black Kettle

60

looked down and raised one eyebrow in a little smile. He and his Cheyenne braves weren't going anywhere.

I turned to Fred and Sam. "But we can't just leave these guys to get wiped out."

"What are we supposed to do?" said Sam. "Take them home with us?"

I looked up and tried to imagine Black Kettle and his warriors in the middle of New York. "I don't know . . ."

"Wait," said Fred. "I've got it. The Time Freezer Spell."

"Oh, right," said Sam. "Just like last time."

"No. Look it up in *The Book*, Mr. Information."

Custer and the Seventh Cavalry were halfway up the hill now and closing in. The braves fired a wave of arrows.

I flipped to the index in the back of *The Book* "Idiot Powder . . . Illness Faking . . . Impossible Acts . . . Industrial Strength Time Freezer Spell—page forty-four."

I thumbed to page 44. The Cheyenne warriors sang and whooped. The Lazy J herd mooed. Custer and the Seventh Cavalry charged.

"So read it, already," said Sam.

"Here goes nothing," I said.

"Hickory Dickory Dock, the mouse ran up the clock.
Hickory Dickory dare, the pig flew up in the air.
Mouse cheese, pig sneeze
Now I command time freeze."

And it did.

Everything stopped.

The cloud of dust hung over the Lazy J herd
like a painting. Custer and his men stood frozen

in mid-charge—puffs of rifle smoke, the curled red-and-white Seventh Cavalry banner, guys with their mouths open, horses on two legs, all as still as if they were made out of stone. Black Kettle and the Cheyenne braves looked like an exhibit from the natural history museum, carefully placed in warlike action poses. And it was absolutely, perfectly, very spookily silent.

Fred, Sam, and I stood up slowly, afraid to break the spell.

"I don't believe it," breathed Sam.

"It really worked," I whispered.

Fred passed his hand in front of Bull Bear's open eyes. Sam walked around a bullet suspended in midair. We turned in circles, studying the weird scene of frozen cowboys, Indians, and cavalry. Sam wiped his glasses on his completely dirty shirt and gave another look to make absolutely sure of what he was seeing. "So now what do we do? Go back home and leave everyone frozen here in 1868?"

"No, I think we have to unfreeze time or it will never make it to our time," I said.

"Why don't we move Black Kettle and his guys out of here," said Fred. "Then we unfreeze time, hop in our green mist, and everybody gets saved." He grabbed Black Kettle's arm and lifted. It didn't budge an inch.

I shook my head. "Frozen in time and space."

"Let me get this straight," said Sam. "We can't unfreeze time because Black Kettle and his guys will get wiped out. But we can't leave time frozen because we won't have a time to go back to, right?"

"Right," I said.

"That's what I was afraid of."

We sat back down on the hill. I tapped my forehead with *The Book*. "Think, you guys. Think." And then I had it. "Of course," I said. And I opened to the index again. "Time Bending . . . Time Folding . . . Time Freezing . . . Time Sliding . . . here it is—Time Unfreezing, page forty-five."

I turned to page 45 and read aloud, " 'Because the Time Freezing Spell puts such a strain on the mechanism of the universe, it should be used only in cases of Extreme Emergency, and even then only once every millennium or so. To unfreeze Time, simply wait. Depending on conditions of the local Time/Space Continuum, Time will usually thaw in fifteen to twenty minutes.' "

"Fifteen to twenty minutes," said Fred, jumping to his feet. "We're almost out of time. Let's get out of here before everybody comes back to life."

"Wait. Here's the part we need—'For Selective

65

Unfreezing, touch the individual person or object to be unfrozen and say *Ezeens sgip, eseehc esuom.*'"

I put my hand on Black Kettle's shoulder and tried it. "*Ezeens sgip, eseehc esuom.*" He blinked, looked around at the frozen scene around us and nodded. "Strong medicine, Joe Magnificent."

Sam and Fred unfroze the rest of the Cheyenne and their ponies while I tried to explain *The Book,* the Industrial Strength Time Freezer Spell, and the thawing of the local time/space continuum to Black Kettle. He didn't seem at all surprised. As each brave came whooping, singing, or screaming to life he called them over.

"Joe Magnificent, Sam Who Tells the Stars, and Warrior Fred have come from time ahead to save us. There are many questions I would like to ask about all of these people." Black Kettle swept his arm in a circle to include cowboys, soldiers, and braves. "But we must leave quickly." Black Kettle jumped on his pony and raised his hand. "As long as the Great Bear walks in the sky we will not forget what you have done for the People."

66

Fred, Sam, and I raised our hands.

The braves walked their ponies carefully past the frozen Seventh Cavalry, holding their bows, rifles, and tomahawks ready. They passed the last bluecoat statue and then took off in a whooping, yelling cloud of dust.

"Good work, Time Warp Medicine Chiefs. Now we just have to time this right to make sure we have a time to go home to," I said.

We heard a great screeching and groaning sound like a giant fingernail dragging across a blackboard and a 70-millimeter Dolby movie soundtrack slowly starting up.

I opened *The Book* to a picture of three guys.

A green mist began to form around our dusty sneakers.

The Lazy J herd came mooing to life and the cavalry resumed its charge.

The mist rose.

Time thawed.

And we were gone.

ELEVEN

You did it," says Cooky. "You stopped Sitting Bull and his Cheyenne. You stopped the stampede. And here comes the cavalry just like you said."

Cowboy Bob pushes back his ten-gallon hat with one of his six-shooters. "I reckon I did, Cooky. Now, why don't you rustle me up a second helping of that good grub. We still got a ways to go down that Old Chillum Trail."

Cowboy Bob and Cooky grin at each other. The music swells. The credits roll up from the bottom of the screen.

AND THAT CONCLUDES TONIGHT'S
"SATURDAY NIGHT AT THE MOVIES" FEATURE,
COWBOY BOB TO THE RESCUE.
BE SURE TO TUNE IN NEXT WEEK FOR
COWBOY BOB WINS THE WEST.

Fred grabbed the remote and clicked off the TV. "Yeah, right."

Fred, Sam, and I looked at each other, still a bit stunned from our trip to the wild West. Our T-shirts, jeans, and sneakers were thoroughly ripped, wrinkled, and covered with dust. Sam tried to straighten his glasses. Fred poked a finger through the hole in his Tigers cap. I tried to decide if my stomach felt the way it did because of beans, bacon, and biscuits or the green time-traveling mist.

"I wonder what happened when those guys got to the top of that hill," said Sam.

I thought about the cavalry, the cowboys, Black Kettle, and his tribe.

"We know what happened to Custer. I wonder whatever happened to Black Kettle and his guys?"

Sam looked out the window and up at the stars. "Well, the Great Bear is still walking up there."

"Shhhh," said Fred. "What's that noise?"

"Oh, no," I said. "Not again."

We froze and listened.

It wasn't a stampede. It wasn't a flash flood.

"Joseph Arthur?"

It was my mom.

Fred, Sam, and I looked at each other and then around the room. We looked and smelled as bad as the Lazy J herd. But the room looked even worse. It was a mother's nightmare of popcorn, soda cans, and us.

The door began to swing slowly open. I imagined the look on my mom's face. I imagined we might have a good case for just one more Extreme Emergency Industrial Strength Time Freezer Spell.

Jon Scieszka collaborated with Lane Smith on the best-selling ALA Notable Book *The True Story of the Three Little Pigs*. He is also the author of *The Frog Prince Continued*, a New York Times Notable Book of 1991. He lives in the present with his wife and two children in Brooklyn. He wanders around the past and future in all sorts of odd places. But wherever he goes, he still pronounces his last name Scieszka (shé-ska).

Lane Smith received a Silver Medal from the Society of Illustrators for *The True Story of the Three Little Pigs* and for *The Big Pets*, which also received a Golden Apple from the Biennale of Illustration Bratislava, and a First Place Award from the New York Book Show. He is the author and illustrator of *Glasses—Who Needs 'em*. His illustrations have appeared in magazines, newspapers, and on record-album covers. He lives in New York City.